Bedtime stories from Winnie-the-Pooh

"I wish to pay tribute to the work of E. H. Shepard
which has been inspirational in the creation
of these new drawings." *Andrew Grey*

EGMONT
We bring stories to life

This edition first published in Great Britain in 2007 by Dean,
an imprint of Egmont UK Limited
239 Kensington High Street, London W8 6SA
Illustrated by Andrew Grey
Based on the 'Winnie-the-Pooh' works
by A. A. Milne and E. H. Shepard
Text © The Trustees of the Pooh Properties
Illustrations © Disney Enterprises, Inc. 2003, 2005
Design © Egmont UK Limited 2007

ISBN 978 0 6035 6274 7
1 3 5 7 9 10 8 6 4 2
Printed in China

Bedtime stories from Winnie-the-Pooh

DEAN

Contents

Pooh Builds
A House

One day when Pooh Bear had nothing else to do, he went round to Piglet's house to see what Piglet was doing. But to his surprise he saw that the door was open, and the more he looked inside the more Piglet wasn't there.

He thought that he would knock very loudly just to make *quite* sure . . . and while he waited, a hum came suddenly into his head . . .

8

The more it snows
(Tiddely pom),
The more it goes
(Tiddely pom),
The more it goes
(Tiddely pom),
On Snowing.
And nobody knows
(Tiddely pom),
How cold my toes
(Tiddely pom),
How cold my toes
(Tiddely pom),
Are growing.

9

"So what I'll do," said Pooh, "is I'll just go home
first and see what the time is, and then I'll go and
see Eeyore and sing it to him."

He hurried back to his own house, and when he
suddenly saw Piglet sitting in his best armchair,
he could only stand there wondering whose house
he was in.

"Hallo, Piglet," he said. "I thought you were out."
"No," said Piglet, "it's *you* who were out, Pooh."
"So it was," said Pooh. "I knew one of us was."

11

POOH BUILDS A HOUSE

"Nearly eleven o'clock," said Pooh, happily. "You're just in time for a little smackerel of something, and then we'll go out and sing my song to Eeyore."

"Which song, Pooh?" asked Piglet.

"The one we're going to sing to Eeyore," explained Pooh.

Half an hour later, Pooh and Piglet set out on their way.

In a little while, Piglet was feeling more snowy behind the ears than he had ever felt before.

"Pooh," he said, a little timidly, because he didn't want Pooh to think he was Giving In. "I was just wondering. How would it be if we went home now and *practised* your song, and then sang it to Eeyore tomorrow?"

"It's no good going home to practise it," said Pooh, "because it's a special Outdoor Song which Has To Be Sung In The Snow. We'll practise it now as we go along."

15

By this time they were getting near Eeyore's Gloomy Place.

"I've been thinking," said Pooh, "poor Eeyore has nowhere to live. So what I've been thinking is this. Let's build him a house."

"That," said Piglet, "is a Grand Idea. Where shall we build it?"

"We will build it here," said Pooh. "And we will call this Pooh Corner."

"I saw a heap of sticks on the other side of the wood," said Piglet.

"Thank you, Piglet," said Pooh. "What you have just said will be a Great Help to us."

And they went round to the other side of the wood to fetch the sticks.

Christopher Robin had spent the morning indoors and was just wondering what it was like outside, when who should come knocking but Eeyore.

"Hallo, Eeyore," said Christopher Robin. "How are *you*?"

"I suppose you haven't seen a house or what-not anywhere about?" said Eeyore.

"Who lives there?" asked Christopher Robin.

"I do. At least I thought I did. But I suppose I don't. After all, we can't all have houses," Eeyore replied.

"Oh, Eeyore!" said Christopher Robin, feeling very sorry.

"I don't know how it is, Christopher Robin," continued Eeyore, "but what with all this snow and one thing and another,

it isn't so Hot in my field about three o'clock in the morning as some people think it is. In fact,

Christopher Robin," he went on in a loud whisper, "quite-between-ourselves-and-don't-tell-anybody, it's Cold."

"Oh, Eeyore!" said Christopher Robin again.

"So what it all comes down to is that I built myself
a house down by my little wood," said Eeyore, in his
most melancholy voice. "But when I came home
today, it wasn't there."

"We'll go and look for it at once," said
Christopher Robin.

And off they hurried, and in a very little time
they got to the corner of the field where Eeyore's
house wasn't any longer.

"There!" said Eeyore. "Not a stick of it left!
Of course, I've still got all this snow to do what
I like with. One mustn't complain."

But Christopher Robin wasn't listening to Eeyore,
he was listening to something else.

"We've finished our HOUSE!"
sang a gruff voice.
"Tiddely pom!"
sang a squeaky one.
"It's a beautiful HOUSE ..."
"Tiddely pom ..."
"I wish it were MINE ..."
"Tiddely pom ..."

"Pooh!" shouted Christopher Robin.

The singers stopped suddenly. "It's Christopher Robin!" said Pooh eagerly.

"He's round by the place where we got all those sticks from," said Piglet.

And they hurried round the corner of the wood, Pooh making **welcoming noises** all the way.

When Christopher Robin had given Pooh a hug, he
began to explain the sad story of Eeyore's Lost
House. And Pooh and Piglet listened, and their eyes
seemed to get bigger and bigger.

"*Where* did you say it was?" asked Pooh.

"Just here," said Eeyore.

"Made of sticks?"

"Yes."

"Oh!" said Piglet, nervously. And so as to seem quite at ease he hummed tiddely-pom once or twice in a **what-shall-we-do-now** kind of way.

"The fact *is*," said Pooh. "Well, the fact *is* . . ."
and he nudged Piglet.

"It's like this . . ." said Piglet. "Only warmer,"
he added, after deep thought.

"What's warmer?"

"The other side of the wood, where Eeyore's
house is," said Piglet.

"*My* house?" said Eeyore. "My house was here."

"No," said Piglet, firmly. "The other side of the wood."

"Because of being warmer," said Pooh.

"Come and look," said Piglet simply, and he led the way.

They came round the corner and there was Eeyore's
house, looking as comfy as anything. Eeyore went
inside . . . and came out again.

"It *is* my house," he said. "And I built it where
I said I did, so the wind must have blown it here.
And here it is as good as ever. In fact, better
in places."

"Much better," said Pooh and Piglet together.
So they left him in it.

Christopher Robin went back to lunch with his friends Pooh and Piglet, and on the way they told him of the **Awful Mistake** they had made. And when he had finished laughing, they all sang the **Outdoor Song** for Snowy Weather the rest of the way home. Piglet, who was still not quite sure of his voice, putting in the **tiddely-poms** again.

"And I know it *seems* easy," said Piglet to himself,
"but it isn't *everyone* who could do it."

31

Pooh Invents
A New Game

One day, Pooh was walking through the Forest, trying to make up a piece of poetry about fir-cones. He picked one up, then this came into his head suddenly:

Here is a myst'ry
About a little fir-tree.
Owl says it's his tree,
And Kanga says it's her tree.

He had just reached a bridge and, not looking where he was going, he **tripped** and the fir-cone jerked out of his paw into the river.

"Bother," said Pooh, as he lay down to watch the river. Suddenly, there was his fir-cone.

"That's funny," said Pooh. "I dropped it on the other side and it came out on this side! I wonder if it would do it again?" And he went back for some more fir-cones.

It did. It kept on doing it. Then he dropped one big one and one little one, and the big one came out first, which was what he had said it would do, and the little one came out last, which was what he had said it would do. So he had won twice.

And that was the beginning of the game called Poohsticks, that Pooh and his friends used to play with sticks instead of fir-cones, because they were easier to mark.

One day, Pooh and Piglet and Rabbit and Roo were playing **Poohsticks**. They had dropped their sticks in when Rabbit said "Go!" and then hurried to the other side of the bridge to see whose stick would come out first.

"I can see mine!" cried Roo. "No, I can't! It's something else. Can you see yours, Pooh?"

"No," said Pooh.

"I expect my stick's stuck," said Roo.

"They always take longer than you think," said Rabbit.

"I can see yours, Piglet," said Pooh, suddenly. "It's coming over to my side."

Piglet got very excited because his was the only one that had been seen, and that meant he was winning.

"Are you *sure* it's mine?" he squeaked, excitedly. "Yes, because it's grey. Here it comes! A very . . . big . . . grey . . . oh, no, it isn't, it's Eeyore."

And out floated Eeyore.

POOH INVENTS A NEW GAME

"Eeyore, what *are* you doing there?" said Rabbit.

"I'll give you three guesses, Rabbit," said Eeyore.

"Digging holes in the ground? Wrong. Leaping from branch to branch of a tree? Wrong. Waiting for somebody to **help me out** of the river? Right."

"But, Eeyore," said Pooh, "what can we . . . I mean, how shall we . . . do you think if we . . ."

"Yes," said Eeyore. "One of those would be **just the thing**. Thank you, Pooh."

"I've got a sort of idea," said Pooh at last, "but I don't suppose it's a very good one."

"Go on, Pooh," said Rabbit.

"Well, if we threw stones into the river on *one* side of Eeyore, the stones would make waves, and the waves would wash him to the other side."

Pooh got a big stone and leant over the bridge.
"I'm not throwing it, I'm dropping it, Eeyore,"
he explained. "And then I can't miss – I mean I
can't hit you."

Pooh dropped his stone. There was a loud splash,
and Eeyore disappeared.

It was an anxious moment for the watchers on
the bridge. Then something grey showed for a
moment by the river bank. It slowly got bigger
and bigger and at last it was Eeyore coming out.
With a shout they rushed off the bridge.

"Well done, Pooh," said Rabbit, kindly. "That was a good idea, hooshing Eeyore to the bank like that."

"*Hooshing* me?" said Eeyore, in surprise. "Pooh dropped a large stone on me, and so as not to be struck heavily on the chest, I dived and swam to the bank."

"How did you **fall in**, Eeyore?" asked Rabbit.

"Somebody **bounced** me. I was just thinking by the side of the river, when I received a **loud bounce**," said Eeyore.

"But who did it?" asked Roo.

"I expect it was Tigger," said Piglet, nervously.

There was a **loud noise** behind them, and through the hedge came Tigger himself.

48

"Hallo, everybody," said Tigger, cheerfully. Rabbit became very important suddenly.

"Tigger," he said. "What happened just now?"

"Just when?" said Tigger.

"When you bounced Eeyore into the river."

"I didn't bounce him. I had a cough, and said,

"That's what I call bouncing," said Eeyore. "Taking people by surprise."

"I didn't bounce, I coughed," said Tigger, crossly. "Bouncy or Coffy, it's all the same at the bottom of the river," said Eeyore.

Christopher Robin came down to the bridge and saw all the animals there.

"It's like this, Christopher Robin," began Rabbit. "Tigger–"

"All I did was I coughed," said Tigger.

"He bounced," said Eeyore.

"Well, I sort of boffed," said Tigger.

"Hush!" said Rabbit. "What does Christopher Robin think about it all? That's the point."

"Well," said Christopher Robin, not quite sure what it was all about. "I think we all ought to play Poohsticks."

So they did. And Eeyore, who had never played it before, won more times than anybody else; and Roo fell in twice, the first time by accident and the second time on purpose, because he saw Kanga coming and knew he'd have to go to bed anyhow.

So then Rabbit said he'd go with them; and Tigger and Eeyore went off together. Christopher Robin and Pooh and Piglet were left on the bridge by themselves.

For a long time they looked at the river beneath them, saying nothing, and the river said nothing too, for it felt very quiet and peaceful on this summer afternoon.

"Tigger is all right, *really*," said Piglet, lazily.

"Of course he is," said Christopher Robin.

"Everybody is *really*," said Pooh. "That's what *I* think, but I don't suppose I'm **right**."

"Of course you are," said Christopher Robin.

Tigger Is Unbounced

One hot summer's day, Rabbit was talking to Pooh and Piglet. Pooh wasn't really listening. From time to time, he opened his eyes to say, "Ah!"

Rabbit said, "You see what I mean, Piglet," and Piglet nodded to show that he did.

"In fact," said Rabbit, "Tigger's getting so bouncy nowadays that it's time we taught him a lesson. Don't you think so, Piglet?"

Piglet agreed Tigger was very bouncy and if they could think of a way of unbouncing him, it would be a Very Good Idea.

"What do *you* say, Pooh?" asked Rabbit.

Pooh opened his eyes and said, "Extremely."

"Extremely what?" asked Rabbit.

"What you were saying," said Pooh. "Undoubtably."

"But how shall we do it?" asked Piglet. "What sort of a lesson?"

"That's the point," said Rabbit.

"What were we talking about?" asked Pooh.

Piglet explained that they were trying to think of a way to get the bounces out of Tigger, because however much you liked him, you couldn't deny it, he did bounce.

"Oh, I see," said Pooh. He tried to think, but he could only think of something which didn't help at all.

So he hummed it very quietly to himself.

If Rabbit
   Was bigger
And fatter
   And stronger,

or bigger
Than Tigger,

If Tigger was smaller,

   Then Tigger's bad habit
Of bouncing at Rabbit

Would matter
No Longer,

If Rabbit
   Was taller.

63

"I've an idea!" said Rabbit. "We take Tigger for a **long explore** and we lose him. The next morning we find him again and he'll be a **different Tigger** altogether. He'll be a Humble Tigger,
a Sad Tigger,
a Melancholy Tigger,
a Small and Sorry Tigger,
an *Oh-Rabbit-I-am-glad-to-see-you* Tigger.
That's why."

"I should hate him to go on being Sad," said Piglet.

"Tiggers never go on being Sad," explained Rabbit. "But if we can make Tigger feel Small and Sad just for **five minutes**, we shall have done a **good deed**."

So the only question was, where should they **lose** Tigger?

64

"We'll take him to the **North Pole**," said Rabbit. "It was a large explore finding it, so it will be a very long explore for Tigger un-finding it again."

Pooh felt glad. It was he who had first found the North Pole so when they got there, Tigger would see a notice saying,

and Tigger would then know what sort of bear he was. **That** sort of bear. So it was arranged that they would start the next morning and Rabbit would go and ask Tigger to come.

The next day was quite a different day. Instead of being sunny, it was cold and misty. Pooh felt sorry for the bees who wouldn't be making honey on such a day.

Piglet wasn't thinking of that, but of how cold and miserable it would be being lost all day and night on top of the Forest on such a day.

Rabbit said it was just the day for them. As soon as Tigger bounced out of sight, they would hurry in the other direction, and he would never see them again.

"Not never?" said Piglet, worriedly.

"Well, not until we find him again," said Rabbit. "Come on. He's waiting for us."

At Kanga's house, they found Roo waiting for them too. This made things **Very Awkward**. Rabbit whispered behind his paw to Pooh, "Leave this to me!"

"Roo had better not come today," he said to Kanga. "He was coughing earlier."

"Oh Roo, you never told me," said Kanga, reproachfully.

"It was a biscuit cough," said Roo. "Not one you tell about."

"I think not today, dear. Another day," Kanga said.

"Ah, Tigger! There you are!" said Rabbit, happily. "All ready? Come on."

So they went.

At first Pooh and Rabbit and Piglet walked together, and Tigger ran round them in circles. Then, when the path got narrower, Rabbit, Piglet and Pooh walked one after another, and Tigger ran round them in oblongs.

When the gorse got very prickly, Tigger ran up and down in front of them, and sometimes bounced into Rabbit.

As they got higher, the mist got thicker, so Tigger kept disappearing, and then bouncing back again. Rabbit nudged Piglet.

"The next time," he said. "Tell Pooh."

"The next what?" said Pooh. Tigger appeared, bounced into Rabbit and disappeared again.

"Now!" said Rabbit. He jumped into a hollow and Pooh and Piglet jumped in after him.

The Forest was silent. They could see nothing and hear nothing.

Then they heard Tigger pattering about.

"Hallo?" he said.

Then they heard him pattering off again.

They waited a little longer and then Rabbit got up. "Well!" he said, proudly. "Just as I said! Come on, let's go!" They all **hurried off**, with Rabbit leading the way.

"Why are we going along here?" said Pooh.

"Because it's **the way home!**" said Rabbit.

"I *think* it's more to the right," said Piglet, nervously. They went on. "Here we are," said Rabbit, ten minutes later. "No, we're not . . ."

"It's a funny thing," said Rabbit, another ten minutes later, "how everything looks the same in a mist. Lucky we know the Forest so well, or we might get lost." Piglet sidled up to Pooh from behind.

"Pooh!" he whispered.

"Yes, Piglet?"

"Nothing," said Piglet, taking Pooh's paw. "I just wanted to be sure of you."

When Tigger had finished **waiting** for the others to catch him up, and they hadn't, he decided he would go home. Kanga gave him a basket and sent him off with Roo to collect fir-cones.

Tigger and Roo threw pine cones at each other until they had quite forgotten what they came for. They left the basket under the trees and went back for dinner.

Just as they were finishing dinner, Christopher Robin put his head around the door and asked,

"Where's Pooh?"

Tigger explained what had happened and Christopher Robin realised Pooh, Piglet and Rabbit were **lost in the mist** on the top of the Forest.

"It's a funny thing about Tiggers," Tigger whispered to Roo, "they never get lost."

"Well," said Christopher Robin to Tigger, "we shall have to go back and find them."

Rabbit, Pooh and Piglet were having a rest in a sandpit. Pooh was **rather tired** of the sandpit, because whichever direction they started in, they always ended up at it again.

"Well," said Rabbit after a while. "We'd better get on. Which way shall we try?"

"How about we leave," said Pooh, "and as soon as we're out of sight of the sandpit, we try to find it again?"

"What's the good of that?" asked Rabbit.

"Well," said Pooh, "we keep looking for Home and not finding it, so if we looked for this pit, we'd be sure not to find it, and we might find something we *weren't* looking for, which might be just what we were looking for really."

"Try," said Piglet to Rabbit, suddenly. "We'll wait here for you."

Rabbit walked into the mist. After Pooh and Piglet had waited twenty minutes for him, Pooh got up.

"Let's go home, Piglet," he said. "There are twelve pots of honey in my cupboard, and they've been calling to me for hours. I couldn't hear them because Rabbit would talk, but if nobody is saying anything then I shall know where they are. Come on."

They walked off together. For a long time Piglet said nothing, then suddenly he made a squeaky noise because now he began to know where he was. Just when he was getting sure, there was a shout and out of the mist came Christopher Robin.

"Oh! There you are," said Christopher Robin carelessly, trying to pretend he hadn't been anxious.

"Here we are," said Pooh.

"Where's Rabbit?" asked Christopher Robin.

"I don't know," said Pooh.

"Oh well, I expect Tigger will find him. He's sort of looking for you all," said Christopher Robin.

"Well," said Pooh, "I've got to go home for *something* and so has Piglet, because we haven't had it yet, and . . ."

"I'll come and watch you," said Christopher Robin.

So he went home with Pooh and watched him for some time.

All the time Christopher Robin was watching Pooh, Tigger was tearing around the Forest making loud yapping noises for Rabbit. And at last, a very Small and Sorry Rabbit heard him. And the Small and Sorry Rabbit rushed through the mist at the noise, and it suddenly turned into Tigger:

a Friendly Tigger,

a Grand Tigger,

a Large and Helpful Tigger,

a Tigger who bounced, if he bounced at all, in just the beautiful way a Tigger ought to bounce.

"Oh, Tigger, **I am glad** to see you," cried Rabbit.

Piglet Does A Very Grand Thing

One windy autumn morning, Pooh and Piglet were sitting in their Thoughtful Spot.

"What *I* think," said Pooh, "is we'll go to Pooh Corner and see Eeyore. In fact, let's go and see everybody."

Piglet thought they ought to have a Reason for seeing everybody if Pooh could think of something. Pooh could.

"We'll go because it's Thursday," he said. "We'll wish everybody a Very Happy Thursday."

By the time they got to Kanga's house they were so buffeted by the wind that they stayed to lunch.

It seemed rather cold outside afterwards, so they pushed on quickly to Rabbit's. "We've come to wish you a **Very Happy Thursday**," said Pooh.

"Oh I thought you'd really come about **something**," Rabbit said. They sat down for a little . . . and by-and-by Pooh and Piglet went on again.

Christopher Robin was so glad to see them that they stayed until very nearly tea time, and had a **Very Nearly** tea. Then they hurried on to Pooh Corner, to see Eeyore before it was too late to have a **Proper Tea** with Owl.

"Hallo, Eeyore. We came to see how your house was," said Piglet. "Look, Pooh, it's still standing!"

"I know," said Eeyore.

"Well, we're very glad to see you, Eeyore, and now we're going on to see Owl," said Pooh.

"Goodbye," said Eeyore. "Mind you don't get blown away, little Piglet."

The **wind**
was against
them now,
and Piglet's ears **streamed**
out behind him like banners.
It seemed like hours
before he got them
into the shelter
of the Hundred
Acre Wood.

In a little while they were knocking and ringing cheerfully at **Owl's door.**

"Hallo, Owl," said Pooh. "I hope we're not too late for . . . I mean, how are you, Owl?"

"Sit down," said Owl, kindly. "Make yourselves comfortable." They made themselves as comfortable as they could.

"Am I right in supposing that it is a **very Blusterous day** outside?" Owl said.

"Very," said Piglet, who was quietly **thawing** his ears.

"I thought so," said Owl. "It was on just such a **Blusterous day** that my Uncle Robert, a portrait of whom you see upon the wall . . . What's that?"

There was a **loud cracking noise.**

"Look out!" cried Pooh. "Piglet, I'm falling on you!" The room was slowly tilting upwards. The clock slithered along the mantelpiece, collecting vases on the way, until they all crashed together on to what had once been the floor, but was now trying to see what it looked like as a wall.

For a little while it became difficult to remember which was really the north. Then there was another loud crack . . . and there was silence.

In the corner of the room,
the table cloth wrapped
itself into a ball
and **rolled** across
the room.

It **jumped** up
and down and
put out two ears.

Then it **unwound**
itself, revealing
Piglet.

"Pooh," said Piglet, nervously. "Are we still in Owl's house?"

"I think so."

"Oh!" said Piglet. "Well, did Owl *always* have a letterbox in his ceiling? Look!"

"I can't," said Pooh. "I'm face downwards under something, and that, Piglet, is a very bad position for looking at ceilings."

Owl and Piglet **pulled** at the chair and in a little while Pooh came out.

"What are we going to do, Pooh?" asked Piglet.

"Well, I *had* just thought of **something**," said Pooh. And he began to sing:

I lay on my chest
And I thought it best
To pretend I was having an evening rest;

I lay on my tum
And I tried to hum
But nothing particular seemed to come.

My face was flat
On the floor, and that
Is all very well for an acrobat;

But it doesn't seem fair
To a Friendly Bear
To stiffen him out with a basket-chair.

And a sort of sqoze
Which grows and grows
Is not too nice for his poor old nose,
And a sort of squch
Is much too much
For his neck and his mouth
and his ears and such.

Owl coughed and said that if Pooh was sure that was all, they could now give their minds to the Problem of Escape.

"Could you fly up to the letterbox with Piglet on your back?" Pooh asked.

"No," said Piglet, quickly. "He couldn't."

Pooh's mind went back to the day when he had saved Piglet from the flood, and everybody had admired him so much. Suddenly, just as it had come before, an idea came to him.

"I have thought of something," said Pooh. "We tie a piece of string to Piglet. Owl flies up to the letterbox, with the other end in his beak, pushes it through the wire and brings it down to the floor. We pull hard at this end, and Piglet goes slowly up at the other end."

"And there he is," said Owl. "If the string doesn't break."

"Supposing it does?" asked Piglet.

"It won't break," whispered Pooh comfortingly, "because you're a Small Animal, and I'll stand underneath, and if you save us all, it will be a Very Grand Thing to talk about afterwards."

Piglet felt **much better**, and when he found himself going up to the ceiling, he was **so proud** that he would have called out 'Look at me!' if he hadn't been **afraid** that Pooh and Owl would let go of their end of the string to look at him.

Soon it
was over.

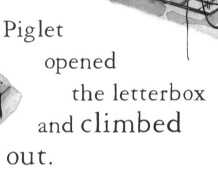

Piglet
    opened
        the letterbox
    and climbed
        out.

He turned to squeak
a last message to
the prisoners.

"It's all right," he called. "Your tree is blown right over, Owl, and there's a branch across the door. I will be back in about half an hour with Christopher Robin. Goodbye, Pooh!" And without waiting to hear Pooh's answering, "Goodbye and thank you," he was off.

"Half an hour," said Owl. "That will just give me time to finish that story I was telling you about my Uncle Robert – a portrait of whom you see underneath you. Now let me see, where was I? Oh, yes. It was on just such a Blusterous day as this that my Uncle Robert . . ."

Pooh closed his eyes.